"BRING THE CLASSICS TO LIFE"

SWISS FAMILY ROBINSON

LEVEL 1

Series Designer
Philip J. Solimene

Editor
Kathryn L. Brennan

EDCON

Long Island, New York

Story Adapter
Mike Guillot

Author
Johann Wyss

About the Author

Johann Rudolf Wyss (Vees) was born in Bern, Switzerland on March 4, 1782 and died in March 1830. His father, Johann David Wyss, wrote the story of Swiss Family Robinson for his family. Johann completed his father's story and had it published. Many people feel that the book is very similar to Daniel Defoe's *Robinson Crusoe*. The younger Johann was a professor and a librarian. In 1811, he wrote the Swiss national anthem.

Copyright © 1997
A/V Concepts Corp.
30 Montauk Blvd, Oakdale NY 11769
info@edconpublishing.com
1-888-553-3266
Visit our Web site at: www.edconpublishing.com

Printed in U.S.A.
ISBN# 1-55576-049-X

CONTENTS

Words Used 4, 5

WORDS USED

Story 31	Story 32	Story 33	Story 34	Story 35
KEY WORDS				
beach	began	boat	idea	daily
found	monkey	hurt	pulled	everywhere
ship	people	our	ready	turtle
swim	running	today	roof	waited
through	sleep	trees	these	watch
NECESSARY WORDS				
loaded	chose	brave	bridge	safe
meal	coconut	careful	easier	seeds
side	hungry	cloth	sick	sight
wife	plenty	floated	stream	supper
	together	lucky	string	worry
		proud		
		sail		
		scared		
		tubs		

WORDS USED

Story 36	Story 37	Story 38	Story 39	Story 40
KEY WORDS				
knew	asked	afternoon	across	apart
light	later	gave	doing	asleep
mud	much	quickly	every	bedroom
nest	smelled	sea	nothing	behind
plants	try	those	part	table
NECESSARY WORDS				
candles	special	learn	canoe	captain
empty	tomorrow	note	cave	changed
sewed		shells	storm	share
smoke				strong
steps				
stung				
winter				

ALONE AT SEA

PREPARATION

Key Words

beach	(bēch)	rocks and sand next to water *I like to run on the <u>beach</u> near my home.*
found	(found)	to get by looking *I <u>found</u> my shoes under my bed.*
ship	(ship)	a large boat *I sailed on a <u>ship</u> across the sea.*
swim	(swim)	to move in water using arms and legs *I <u>swim</u> in my pool when it is warm.*
through	(thro͞o)	in one side and out the other side of *The dog went <u>through</u> the door into the house.*

ALONE AT SEA

Necessary Words

loaded   (lōd ed)   put on or put in; filled up
We <u>loaded</u> up the wagon with all our toys.

meal   (mēl)   food
The <u>meal</u> he fixed for us was very good.

side   (sīd)   a wall, going from top to bottom; not the front, the back, the top or the bottom
I will meet you by the <u>side</u> door.

wife   (wīf)   a married woman
"This is my <u>wife</u>, Mrs. Jones," said Mr. Jones.

ALONE AT SEA

We held on to each other during the storm. What would we do? Would we ever get to land?

Preview:	1. Read the name of the story.
	2. Look at the picture.
	3. Read the sentences under the picture.
	4. Read the first paragraph of the story.
	5. Then answer the following question.

You learned from your preview that
___ a. the Robinsons were having a party.
___ b. the Robinsons were no longer together.
___ c. the Robinsons did not like each other.
___ d. the ship the Robinsons were on hit a big rock.

Turn to the Comprehension Check on page 10 for the right answer.

Now read the story.

Read to find out what happens to the Robinsons on their search for a new home.

ALONE AT SEA

My name is Robinson. I and Mrs. Robinson were on a ship at sea with our four sons. We were going to a new land, and we were happy. One night, the rain fell hard. The wind blew hard. The water pushed our ship too fast. We were afraid. The men on our ship left in small boats. We were alone. The ship hit a big rock and could not move. Now we felt very afraid. The animals on the ship were afraid. As night went on, the rain still fell, and the wind still blew. We could not sleep.

When morning came, we could see through the rain that our ship had a big crack in its side. Water was slowly coming into the ship. I could also see land from our ship. A beach was near. We hoped that once the rain stopped, we could swim to the beach. That night, we ate our last meal on the ship. Fritz, our oldest boy, said, "Father, only you and I can swim. How will Mother and my three brothers get to the beach?" I did not know what to do.

When we woke up, the rain and wind had stopped. I sent everyone to look through the ship. They looked for things we could use on land. Fritz and little Franz found some things to catch animals. Ernest found some things to build a house. My wife found a surprise. Some cows and other animals were still well. Jack found two dogs. We also found some boxes that could hold these things and the people who could not swim. We loaded the boxes. "Let's go!" I said. We left the ship and made our way to the beach. I thought to myself, "Would we make it?"

ALONE AT SEA

COMPREHENSION CHECK

Choose the best answer.

1. The Robinson family
   ___a. was going to a new land.
   ___b. was going home.
   ___c. was going to find elephants.
   ___d. was going to a baseball game.

2. While on the ship, a storm came along. All the men on the ship
   ___a. started to cry.
   ___b. told Mr. Robinson not to be afraid.
   ___c. left the ship in small boats.
   ___d. stayed with the Robinson family.

3. Through the rain, the Robinsons
   ___a. could see other ships in the water.
   ___b. could see a big crack in the boat.
   ___c. could see nothing.
   ___d. could hear airplanes.

4. Mr. Robinson knew their only hope was to swim to land, but
   ___a. everyone wanted to stay on the ship.
   ___b. he could not swim.
   ___c. he did not see any land near.
   ___d. his wife and three of his sons could not swim.

5. When the rain stopped, everyone went looking through the ship for
   ___a. more people.
   ___b. more cookies.
   ___c. things they could use on land.
   ___d. Grandmother and Grandfather.

6. On the ship, Fritz and Franz found
   ___a. some things to catch animals.
   ___b. Grandmother.
   ___c. nothing.
   ___d. candy.

7. Ernest found
   ___a. nothing.
   ___b. Grandfather.
   ___c. things to build a house.
   ___d. his pet dog.

8. The things and people that could not swim
   ___a. were left on the ship.
   ___b. tried to swim anyway.
   ___c. waited for another ship to come get them.
   ___d. were put into boxes that would carry them in the water.

9. Another name for this story could be
   ___a. "The Rains."
   ___b. "Home At Last!"
   ___c. "Never Again."
   ___d. "A Great Day."

10. This story is mainly about
    ___a. learning to swim.
    ___b. a family on a sea trip to a new land.
    ___c. four boys fighting.
    ___d. what to do on a ship when it rains.

Check your answers with the key on page 67.

ALONE AT SEA

VOCABULARY CHECK

beach	found	ship	swim	through

I. Sentences to Finish

Fill in the blank in each sentence with the correct key word from the box above.

1. Mom is going to show me how to _____ .

2. The _____ will take us across the sea to a new land.

3. We go to the _____ in the summer.

4. I could hear the noise from the next room _____ the walls.

5. Has anyone _____ my little lost kitten?

II. Making Sense of Sentences

Put a check next to YES if the sentence makes sense. Put a check next to NO if the sentence does not make sense.

1. At the <u>beach</u>, the ground is covered with grass and snow. ___ YES ___ NO

2. If I <u>found</u> my shoes, I got them by looking for them. ___ YES ___ NO

3. A <u>ship</u> is a small stone. ___ YES ___ NO

4. To learn to <u>swim</u>, you must put boots on. ___ YES ___ NO

5. When you go <u>through</u> something, you go in one side and out the other. ___ YES ___ NO

Check your answers with the key on page 69.

WE MADE IT

PREPARATION

Key Words

began	(bi gan´)	past tense of begin; started; came into being
		When he dropped his toy, the boy <u>began</u> to cry.
monkey	(mun´ kē)	small, long-tailed animal
		The <u>monkey</u> at the zoo is friendly.
people	(pē´p´ l)	persons
		A lot of <u>people</u> go to my school.
running	(run´ing)	moving quickly on your feet
		The children were <u>running</u> in the yard.
sleep	(slēp)	rest with eyes closed, not moving
		I <u>sleep</u> in a nice, soft bed.

WE MADE IT

Necessary Words

chose   (chōz)   picked out
> *I <u>chose</u> the ice cream, not the cookies.*

coconut   (kō´ kə nŭt´)   a fruit; a large seed that has a thick, hard shell. Inside a coconut is white meat and milk.
> *Mother went to the store and brought us back a <u>coconut</u>.*

hungry   (hung´grē)   feeling a need for food
> *I must get something to eat, I am so <u>hungry</u>.*

plenty   (plen´tē)   a large amount
> *There are <u>plenty</u> of apples in that basket.*

together   (tə geTH´ er)   with each other; at the same time; not apart
> *We can go to the party <u>together</u> if you like.*

WE MADE IT

We used everything we could find that would float.
We took the animals, some supplies, and ourselves to the new land.

Preview: 1. Read the name of the story.
2. Look at the picture.
3. Read the sentences under the picture.
4. Read the first paragraph of the story.
5. Then answer the following question.

You learned from your preview that
___ a.   another ship came by and saved everyone.
___ b.   the Robinson family was safe, together, and happy.
___ c.   Fritz was lost.
___ d.   the Robinsons never made it to land.

Turn to the Comprehension Check on page 16 for the right answer.

Now read the story.

Read to find out what the Robinsons find on the new land.

WE MADE IT

We rode in our boxes. We went close to some rocks. When we made it to land, my wife, my sons, and I thanked God. We were safe, we were together, and we were happy.

We began to get hungry. Mother cooked some food from the ship. The boys went running to look for fish. Then I heard Jack cry, "Papa, Papa, help me!" Something had bitten his foot. I reached into the water. What a surprise! It was a big fish. We put it in the pot.

Fritz came back. He had found no people on this land. He said, "There is plenty to see." We ate our food. We made a place to rest, and we went to sleep.

It was morning. Fritz and I left the beach with one of the dogs. We began looking for other people. Fritz asked, "May I make a loud noise?" I said, "No. Someone bad might answer." We looked. We found no one. We did find some good things to eat. We saw one monkey in a tree. Then we saw many monkeys in a tree. We threw rocks at them. To our surprise, they threw coconuts at us. We took the coconuts. A baby monkey stayed with Fritz. We went back to the beach.

That night, we ate some fish. When the sun went down, we fell asleep. In the night, the dogs barked. Something was wrong. When we woke up, we saw many bad animals running at us. We were scared. What would we do?

WE MADE IT

COMPREHENSION CHECK

Choose the best answer.

1. When they were looking for fish, Jack cried out for his father because
   ___a. something had bitten his foot.
   ___b. he wanted to go home.
   ___c. the boat was tipping over.
   ___d. he was getting all wet.

2. Fritz said that even though there were no other people on the land,
   ___a. there were a lot of houses.
   ___b. there were a lot of cars.
   ___c. there was plenty to see.
   ___d. there was an airport.

3. Father told Fritz not to make any loud noises because
   ___a. he would wake someone.
   ___b. someone bad might answer.
   ___c. the people on the land did not like noise.
   ___d. he did not feel well.

4. When Father and Fritz went out looking for other people, they saw
   ___a. many dogs.
   ___b. many people.
   ___c. a bus station.
   ___d. monkeys.

5. First, Fritz threw rocks at the monkeys in the trees. Then,
   ___a. Fritz went up the tree.
   ___b. the monkeys threw food at them.
   ___c. the monkeys ran away.
   ___d. the monkeys chased them away.

6. Not only did Fritz take food back to Mother, he also took back
   ___a. the people he found.
   ___b. some beautiful butterflies.
   ___c. a baby monkey.
   ___d. a set of new dishes.

7. At the end of this story, when everyone was sleeping, the dogs started to bark. Why?
   ___a. Bad animals were coming after the Robinson family.
   ___b. The dogs wanted food.
   ___c. The dogs wanted to play.
   ___d. The dogs wanted to be let free.

8. The dogs had barked to let the Robinsons know
   ___a. they were hungry.
   ___b. about the danger.
   ___c. they wanted to play.
   ___d. they were cold.

9. Another name for this story could be
   ___a. "Safe on Land."
   ___b. "A Rainy Day."
   ___c. "The Picnic."
   ___d. "The Red Ladder."

10. This story is mainly about
   ___a. learning to swim.
   ___b. animals at the zoo.
   ___c. how to plant a garden.
   ___d. the Robinsons' first days in a new land.

Check your answers with the key on page 67.

This page may be reproduced for classroom use.

WE MADE IT

VOCABULARY CHECK

| began | monkey | people | running | sleep |

I.   Sentences to Finish

Fill in the blank in each sentence with the correct key word from the box above.

1. The teacher told us to stop _____ in the hall.

2. The small, long-tailed animal in the tree was a _____ .

3. How many _____ will be coming to your party?

4. It is late and I am tired. I think I will go to _____ .

5. The rain _____ to fall just as I went out the door.

II.   Word Search

All the words from the box above are hidden in the puzzle below. They may be written from left to right or up and down. As you find each word, put a circle around it. One word, that is not a key word, has been done for you.

```
H   L   S   B   D   K   J   M
M   O   N   K   E   Y   X   P
B   E   G   A   N   S   V   E
O   J   K   B   D   L   Z   O
M   C  (L   O   T)  E   T   P
S   V   D   D   T   E   Q   L
U   W   F   Q   U   P   R   E
T   R   U   N   N   I   N   G
```

Check your answers with the key on page 69.

This page may be reproduced for classroom use.

A NEW HOME

PREPARATION

Key Words

boat   (bōt)   a small ship
             My dad rowed a <u>boat</u> on the lake.

hurt   (hûrt)   to feel or cause pain
             I <u>hurt</u> my finger in the door.

our   (our)   belonging to us
             <u>Our</u> team is playing tonight.

today   (tə dā)   the present day
             I am going shopping <u>today</u>.

trees   (trēz)   tall, woody plants
             There are many <u>trees</u> in a forest.

A NEW HOME

Necessary Words

brave	(brāv)	faces danger with courage; having no fear
		The lady thanked me for being so <u>brave</u> and for helping her.
careful	(kār´fəl)	watchful, looking out
		Always be <u>careful</u> when crossing the street.
cloth	(klŏth)	fabric
		My <u>cloth</u> coat keeps me warm.
floated	(flōt ed)	stayed on top of the water
		The boat <u>floated</u> on the water.
lucky	(lŭk ē)	having good things happen
		I won the prize. I felt very <u>lucky</u>.
proud	(proud)	feeling good about something
		I am <u>proud</u> of myself for getting an "A" on the test.
sail	(sāl)	a cloth to catch the wind
		We watched the little boat <u>sail</u> on the lake.
scared	(skārd)	afraid; not feeling safe
		I was so <u>scared</u>, I started to cry.
tubs	(tŭbz)	containers
		At the dairy farm, they keep butter in <u>tubs</u>.

A NEW HOME

Father and Fritz must go back to the ship to get some things they need for their new home.

Preview:	1. Read the name of the story.
	2. Look at the picture.
	3. Read the sentence under the picture.
	4. Read the first paragraph of the story.
	5. Then answer the following question.

You learned from your preview that the Robinsons had to fight with bad animals and

___ a. no one was hurt.
___ b. Fritz ran away.
___ c. mother cried.
___ d. everyone was hurt bad.

Turn to the Comprehension Check on page 22 for the right answer.

Now read the story.

Read to find out how Father brings back the things they need.

A NEW HOME

Some bad animals came at us. We had to fight them. Our dogs barked. The boys and I hit the bad animals. We scared the bad animals away. We were lucky no one was hurt.

We were proud of our brave dogs. Jack said, "I am glad we took these dogs with us." Then we went back to bed.

In the morning, I said to my wife, "Today, Fritz and I will go back to the ship. We must go before a bad rain comes. Fritz and I will look through the ship for animals. We will look for more food." My wife said, "Be careful. I don't want you to get hurt."

We floated in our tubs back to the ship. We found some cloth on the ship, so we made a sail for our little boat. Then, we found some food. We found some more things we could use. We put everything on our little boat and looked some more.

We found some good animals on the ship. Fritz asked, "How will the animals get to the beach?" I said, "They will float. We must find some things to help them." We used some tubs. We used anything that would float. We put the animals in the water. It worked; our boat made it to the beach. The animals made it to the beach. Our family was happy to see us.

We put away the new things. We took care of the animals. Then we ate supper. It was very good, and we all had plenty to eat. I was happy.

Mother said, "We need a new home; the beach is too hot. The boys and I looked around today. We found some tall trees. We could live under these trees. Can we move?"

I was surprised. Mother was right, we should have a new home. I said, "Yes, we will start in the morning." We went to sleep happy about our new home.

A NEW HOME

COMPREHENSION CHECK

Choose the best answer.

1. The Robinsons hit the bad animals and
   ___a. threw eggs at them.
   ___b. they ran back into the house.
   ___c. scared the animals away.
   ___d. ate them for breakfast.

2. The dogs saved the Robinsons from danger and
   ___a. they were given more food.
   ___b. they were put back in cages.
   ___c. the Robinsons gave the dogs a bath.
   ___d. the Robinsons were proud of their dogs.

3. Father and Fritz wanted to go back to the ship
   ___a. before the rains came.
   ___b. and sink it.
   ___c. and go back home.
   ___d. to get the elephant.

4. On the ship, Father and Fritz looked for
   ___a. gold.
   ___b. animals and food.
   ___c. money.
   ___d. a radio.

5. Fritz and Father found things on the ship that they could use back at the beach, so they
   ___a. put as much as they could in their little boat.
   ___b. took the ship to the beach.
   ___c. called for help.
   ___d. asked the captain if they could have the things.

6. How did they get the animals back to the beach?
   ___a. They put them all on the little boat.
   ___b. They carried them.
   ___c. They just threw them into the water.
   ___d. They put them into tubs and anything else that would float.

7. Mother told Father that
   ___a. they needed a new home.
   ___b. she loved the beach.
   ___c. they should cut down the trees.
   ___d. she wanted to sail home.

8. As long as the Robinson family was together, they were happy. They
   ___a. were always fighting with each other.
   ___b. made the most out of whatever happened to them.
   ___c. yelled at one another all the time.
   ___d. would not help one another.

9. Another name for this story could be
   ___a. "Happy Birthday."
   ___b. "A Sad Time."
   ___c. "The Circus."
   ___d. "Back to the Ship."

10. This story is mainly about
    ___a. many kinds of animals.
    ___b. a family fighting.
    ___c. a family working together.
    ___d. animals learning to swim.

Check your answers with the key on page 67.

This page may be reproduced for classroom use.

A NEW HOME

VOCABULARY CHECK

boat	hurt	our	today	trees

I. Sentences to Finish

Fill in the blank in each sentence with the correct key word from the box above.

1. _____ family has five people in it.

2. I _____ my foot when I fell.

3. We have many tall _____ growing in our yard.

4. It is my birthday _____ .

5. We all went for a ride on the lake in a _____ .

II. Matching

Write the letter of the correct meaning from Column B next to the key word in Column A.

Column A

1. our   _____

2. trees   _____

3. hurt   _____

4. boat   _____

5. today   _____

Column B

a. to feel pain

b. a small ship

c. belonging to us

d. the present day

e. tall, woody plants

Check your answers with the key on page 69.

OUR TREE HOUSE

PREPARATION

Key Words

idea	(ī dēa)	a useful thought *I have an <u>idea</u> about our picnic.*
pulled	(po͝old)	moved toward with force *I <u>pulled</u> the door open.*
ready	(rĕd ē)	be prepared *I am <u>ready</u> for school.*
roof	(ro͞of)	the top covering of a building *That <u>roof</u> has a red chimney.*
these	(thēz)	two or more things present or spoken of *<u>These</u> dolls are beautiful.*

OUR TREE HOUSE

Necessary Words

bridge   (brij)   a walkway or road that is built to go across water, a railroad, etc., for people to get from one side to the other
We drove our car across the <u>bridge</u>.

easier   (ē´zē ĕr)   less difficult; not as hard as
Every time I play baseball it gets <u>easier</u>.

sick   (sĭk)   not feeling well
Mom stayed home from work today because she is <u>sick</u>.

stream   (strēm)   running water
We put our feet in the <u>stream</u> and the water was cold.

string   (string)   very thin rope; a very thick thread
I need a piece of <u>string</u> to tie this box.

OUR TREE HOUSE

Everyone, even the animals, helped with the bridge.

Preview:
1. Read the name of the story.
2. Look at the picture.
3. Read the sentence under the picture.
4. Read the first paragraph of the story.
5. Then answer the following question.

You learned from your preview that the Robinsons
___ a. must build a bridge.
___ b. are going to the beach.
___ c. are going hunting.
___ d. are going swimming.

Turn to the Comprehension Check on page 28 for the right answer.

Now read the story.

Read to find out where the Robinsons build their new home.

OUR TREE HOUSE

It was morning, and we were ready to move. We would have a new home in a big tree. First we must build a bridge. This bridge would cross a stream.

The boys found some wood on the beach. This wood was just right for our bridge. We brought the wood to the stream. Some of the animals helped. We worked hard. That night, we finished the bridge and were ready to move.

The next day, we began moving to our new home. The animals pulled some things. We came to the new bridge. It held us. We were very proud of our work.

Soon we were at our new home. The giant trees were beautiful. It was not hot here; not like the beach. That night, we slept by the trees. We felt happy.

In the morning I said to my family, "I have an idea. We will build our home high up in this tree. We will be safe from bad animals. It will be hard work, and it will take us a long time." We were ready to start.

We pulled some wood up the tree. We made a floor in the branches; we built walls on the floor. We even made a roof. The roof would keep out the rain. At night, we would be safer than ever. It was good.

I built a wagon. The wagon made it easier to carry our things. We went back to the beach to get our things and bring them back to the tree house. We were happy about our new home.

We found some new things to eat. These things were very good. Then we found another plant that could make you feel better if you were sick. Our new home was getting better.

We saw some ducks that were from the ship. They would not come to us. Ernest had an idea. He tied some food to a string. The ducks liked the food. He pulled the string and caught the ducks.

I looked at our new home; it was beautiful. But we still needed some things. Fritz and I must go back to the ship.

OUR TREE HOUSE

COMPREHENSION CHECK

Choose the best answer.

1. The Robinsons are going to live
    ___a. on a boat.
    ___b. under a bridge.
    ___c. in an apartment.
    ___d. in a tree.

2. To get to their new house, the Robinsons had to
    ___a. take a train.
    ___b. take a plane.
    ___c. cross over a stream.
    ___d. get on another ship.

3. The new home would be
    ___a. hot.
    ___b. safer than the beach.
    ___c. hard to live in.
    ___d. not safe at all.

4. Dad's idea was to
    ___a. build a home high up in the tree.
    ___b. go back to the beach.
    ___c. go to another land.
    ___d. go back to live on the ship.

5. Dad and the boys pulled some wood up the tree
    ___a. to hide from mother.
    ___b. to hide from the ducks.
    ___c. to use as floors.
    ___d. to build a fire.

6. The things they took from the ship
    ___a. were used to build the tree house.
    ___b. were washed away.
    ___c. were of no use.
    ___d. caught on fire.

7. With the things from the ship, Father also built
    ___a. a garage.
    ___b. a wagon.
    ___c. a car.
    ___d. an apartment building.

8. Why did Ernest catch the ducks?
    ___a. He wanted a pet.
    ___b. He wanted to put them in the sea.
    ___c. He was just having fun.
    ___d. He wanted his family to have food.

9. Another name for this story could be
    ___a. "The Circus."
    ___b. "Hello Again."
    ___c. "A Sad Good-by."
    ___d. "A Safe Home."

10. This story is mainly about
    ___a. a lost dog.
    ___b. an unhappy family.
    ___c. a family building a home.
    ___d. how to cut down trees.

Check your answers with the key on page 67.

OUR TREE HOUSE

VOCABULARY CHECK

idea	pulled	ready	roof	these

I.   Sentences to Finish

Fill in the blank in each sentence with the correct key word from the box above.

1. My sister is in her room getting _____ for the party.

2. We have to have our _____ fixed because it has a hole in it.

3. I have no _____ what to give her for her birthday.

4. Who wants _____ last two cookies?

5. My brother _____ the wagon up the hill.

II.   Crossword Puzzle

Use the words from the box above to fill in the puzzle. The meanings below help you choose the right words.

Across

1. moved toward with force
3. prepared

Down

1. two or more things present
2. a useful thought
3. the top of a building

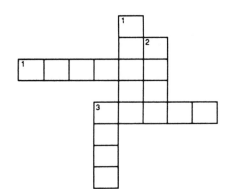

Check your answers with the key on page 70.

This page may be reproduced for classroom use.

CTR A-35

BACK TO THE SHIP

PREPARATION

Key Words

daily	(dā´ lē)	happening every day *I get the newspaper <u>daily</u>.*
everywhere	(ĕv´rē hwâr´)	in every place *I looked <u>everywhere</u> for my lost puppy.*
turtle	(tûrt´l)	an animal with a large shell covering its body *The <u>turtle</u> pulls its head in when afraid.*
waited	(wāt ed)	remained still *We <u>waited</u> for the start of the race.*
watch	(wŏch)	to look at carefully *<u>Watch</u> the house while we're gone.*
		something you wear on your wrist to tell time *I left my <u>watch</u> home and I do not know what time it is.*

BACK TO THE SHIP

Necessary Words

safe   (sãf)   not harmful or dangerous
                              You will be <u>safe</u> here with us.

seeds   (sĕds)   a plant's beginning
                              John planted <u>seeds</u> in the garden.

sight   (sīt)   thing seen; power of seeing
                              I lost <u>sight</u> of my balloon once I let it go.

supper   (sŭp´ər)   the evening meal
                              We eat <u>supper</u> at six o'clock.

worry   (wûr´ē)   bother; trouble
                              Do not <u>worry</u> about me, I will be fine.

BACK TO THE SHIP

We found some seeds for food and trees.   We put them in our boat with the other things.

Preview: 1. Read the name of the story.
2. Look at the picture.
3. Read the sentences under the picture.
4. Read the first paragraph of the story.
5. Then answer the following question.

You learned from your preview that Fritz and his father
___ a. had a big fight.
___ b. went back home.
___ c. did not like each other.
___ d. went back to the ship.

Turn to the Comprehension Check on page 34 for the right answer.

Now read the story.

Read to find out about all the things they found on the ship.

BACK TO THE SHIP

Fritz and I went back to the ship. Our first job was to find some more things to use. We must hurry to get these things now. A bad rain may come any time. We looked everywhere. We took everything we could. We took windows and doors and some beds. Fritz and I slept on the ship that night.

We got lucky in the morning when we found some seeds for trees and food. We took them from the ship. We put everything on our boat and went back to the beach.

On the way, Fritz said, "I see something in the water. Let's go look." What he had seen was a big turtle. We caught it. It was so big, it pulled the boat. The turtle would be a good supper that evening.

The whole family waited for us on the beach. They were glad to see us. Everyone helped move our new things. Soon, we were safe in our tree house.

After supper, I said, "Boys, we must go back to the ship. I saw the wood to build a new boat. Our new boat **will** be big and safe." The boys were happy. Mother said, "I worry about you on that ship. Franz and I will stay on the beach. We can watch you almost everywhere on the ship. I will feel better." I said yes, and we went to sleep.

In the morning, we went back to the ship. We had hard work to do. Daily, the boys took wood from a wall of the ship. The work took many days. Each night, we would go back to the beach. Mother and Franz were there with supper ready. Daily, we would go back to the ship, and Mother would watch us.

More days went by. At last, our new boat was ready. But how to get it out of the ship? I had an idea. We would blow up a side of the ship. I set the fire. The boys and I ran to our tubs. We left as fast as we could. Then, "Boooom!" We waited. Had it worked? We went back to the ship.

It worked! What a beautiful sight. There was a big hole in the ship. We pulled our new boat out. It was great. We surprised Mother and Franz. We came home in a new, big boat. Mother was very proud of us.

Then Mother said, "Come see. I have a surprise for you."

What could it be?

BACK TO THE SHIP

COMPREHENSION CHECK

Choose the best answer.

1. Father and Fritz went back to the ship
    ___a. to run away.
    ___b. to get more things to use.
    ___c. to live on it.
    ___d. to bring it closer to land.

2. On the ship, they found
    ___a. Mother.
    ___b. the ship's captain.
    ___c. seeds.
    ___d. gold.

3. On the way back to the beach, Fritz and Father found
    ___a. more sand.
    ___b. another land.
    ___c. a balloon.
    ___d. a big turtle.

4. Father wanted to go back to the ship again because
    ___a. he saw some wood he could use to build a new boat.
    ___b. he liked to stay on the ship.
    ___c. the captain told him to come back.
    ___d. he was tired of sleeping in the tree house.

5. Mother and Franz went to stay on the beach because
    ___a. Mother didn't like the tree house.
    ___b. Mother wanted to get away from everyone.
    ___c. Mother wanted to go fishing.
    ___d. Mother wanted to be able to watch Father and Fritz on the ship.

6. During the day, Father and the boys would work on the ship. At night, they would sleep on the beach. Why?
    ___a. They were having fun.
    ___b. They had nothing else to do.
    ___c. Mrs. Robinson and Franz waited there for them.
    ___d. They didn't like to sleep on the ship.

7. When the new boat was ready, how did they get it out of the ship?
    ___a. They threw it into the water.
    ___b. They blew open a side of the ship.
    ___c. They just dropped it into the water.
    ___d. They opened the doors and pulled it out.

8. Mother was proud of Father and the boys because
    ___a. they worked hard and did a good job.
    ___b. they blew up the ship.
    ___c. they won the race.
    ___d. they were doing well in school.

9. Another name for this story could be
    ___a. "The Surprise Party."
    ___b. "No Work Today."
    ___c. "Forever Yours."
    ___d. "The New Boat."

10. This story is mainly about
    ___a. a family working together.
    ___b. turtles.
    ___c. buying wood for a boat.
    ___d. people that do not get along with each other.

Check your answers with the key on page 67.

BACK TO THE SHIP

VOCABULARY CHECK

daily	everywhere	turtle	waited	watch

I. *Sentences to Finish*

Fill in the blank in each sentence with the correct key word from the box above.

1. The _____ walked across the road very slowly.

2. We get the _____ newspaper each morning.

3. Mother asked me to _____ my baby sister for an hour.

4. I have looked _____ for my shoes and I still can't find them.

5. My dog _____ by the front door for me to come home.

II. *Mixed-up Words*

First, unscramble the letters in Column A to spell out the key words. Then, match the key words with the right meaning in Column B by drawing a line.

Column A

1. thacw _____

2. lutter _____

3. awidet _____

4. laidy _____

5. wheyreveer _____

Column B

a. in every place

b. happening every day

c. to look at carefully

d. remained still

e. an animal with a large shell covering its body

Check your answers with the key on page 70.

GETTING READY FOR WINTER

PREPARATION

Key Words

knew	(nyü)	past tense of know; to have been aware of *I knew you when I was a child.*
light	(līt)	brightness in order to see *Sam needs plenty of light for reading.*
mud	(mŭd)	soft, wet earth *I'll never get all the mud off my shoes.*
nest	(nĕst)	a place for young animals *We found a nest of eggs on a nature walk.*
plant(s)	(plănt(s))	green, living thing(s) *Grandmother waters her plants in the morning.*

GETTING READY FOR WINTER

Necessary Words

candles	(kăn´- dəls)	sticks made of wax that give off light when lit *The only light in the room is coming from the <u>candles</u> on his birthday cake.*
empty	(ĕmp´- tē)	nothing inside *The box was <u>empty</u>; someone had taken every-thing out.*
sewed	(sōd)	used a needle and a thread to make or fix some-thing *I <u>sewed</u> up the hole in my dress.*
smoke	(smōk)	clouds from a fire *I could not see through the <u>smoke</u>.*
steps	(stĕps)	stairs *Never leave toys or things on the <u>steps</u>; some-one could fall on them.*
stung	(stŭng)	stuck by a sharp point *The bee <u>stung</u> me.*
winter	(win´tər)	the coldest time of the year, the time between fall and spring *I wear a heavy coat to keep warm in the <u>winter</u>.*

GETTING READY FOR WINTER

Franz got stung by the bees. We must get rid of them.

> **Preview:**   1. Read the name of the story.
> 2. Look at the picture.
> 3. Read the sentences under the picture.
> 4. Read the first paragraph of the story.
> 5. Then answer the following question.
>
> You learned from your preview that
> ___ a. it was summer.
> ___ b. Father and Fritz never came back.
> ___ c. everyone would have plenty to eat.
> ___ d. Father and Fritz were hungry.
>
> *Turn to the Comprehension Check on page 40 for the right answer.*

Now read the story.

Read to find out about the new steps for the tree house.

GETTING READY FOR WINTER

Mother and Franz had a surprise for us. We had built the new boat; they had made a garden. It was filled with good food. We knew we would have plenty to eat.

Fritz and I looked around our new home. We found some new plants. We could use these plants for candles. We found something wet from a tree. It was good for filling holes. That night, we made some candles. It worked. We had light at night. I could read aloud to my boys by the light.

The next day, Mother asked a question. "Can we have steps for our tree house?" I thought about it and said, "Not outside. But, maybe inside the tree trunk."

I called for Franz. "Franz," I said, "Did you see bees?" Franz said, "Yes, Papa. I will show you the nest." Franz showed me the hole in the tree. "That is good," I said. "Bees live inside the tree. This tree is empty inside. We can make the steps inside the tree trunk."

The bees did not like Franz. They left their nest and flew at him. They stung him. We took care of Franz. Fritz and I closed the hole with mud. I put some smoke into the tree, and the bees went to sleep. We took the bees from the tree and put them into a tub. I said, "The bees are happy here. They will make honey."

Then we went to work on the steps. We cut a big hole in the tree. We had a door from the ship so we put the door into the big hole. Mother went inside and she said, "I can see the sky." We would build the steps. The steps would be inside the tree.

We then made some windows. We cut holes in the side of the tree then put the windows inside the holes. It was hard work, and it took many days, but we were proud of the steps.

Next, we built a new place for our animals. They wanted a home, too. We also put our food there. I knew winter was coming very soon.

The rain started. It was a hard rain. It rained and rained. There was mud everywhere. We stayed inside the tree and kept busy. Ernest drew pictures of animals. Fritz taught Franz to read. Mother sewed. I began to write this story.

GETTING READY FOR WINTER

COMPREHENSION CHECK

Choose the best answer.

1. When Fritz and Father came back from the ship, there was a surprise waiting for them. What was it?
   ___a. The ship's captain was there.
   ___b. A new ship had landed.
   ___c. It was raining.
   ___d. Mother had planted a garden.

2. Father and Fritz found some plants and made
   ___a. candles from them.
   ___b. a garden.
   ___c. a basket.
   ___d. a fire.

3. Mother asked Father if
   ___a. she could have a new car.
   ___b. she could go home.
   ___c. they could have steps for the tree house.
   ___d. they could live in an apartment house.

4. When they were building steps inside the tree, what happened to Franz?
   ___a. He was stung by bees.
   ___b. He broke his leg.
   ___c. He fell in love.
   ___d. He was sent to his room.

5. Because the Robinsons had to get the bees out of the tree to build steps, they
   ___a. cut the tree down.
   ___b. put smoke into the tree and closed up the hole with mud.
   ___c. put honey in a tub so the bees would follow it.
   ___d. blew a hole in the side of the tree and the bees flew out.

6. Not only did the Robinson family put steps in the tree house, they also put in
   ___a. a swimming pool.
   ___b. an elevator.
   ___c. a door and windows.
   ___d. a basketball net.

7. The Robinsons also built a new place for their animals. Why?
   ___a. To keep them safe in the winter.
   ___b. They wanted to build a zoo.
   ___c. The animals liked the indoors.
   ___d. The animals were afraid of the dark.

8. To keep busy during the winter, Mr. Robinson
   ___a. went swimming.
   ___b. played baseball.
   ___c. took a nap.
   ___d. started to write this story.

9. Another name for this story could be
   ___a. "Mud Everywhere."
   ___b. "The Garden."
   ___c. "Working Hard."
   ___d. "New Plants."

10. This story is mainly about
   ___a. making a swimming hole.
   ___b. making a boat.
   ___c. how all alone the Robinsons felt.
   ___d. how the Robinsons got their tree house ready for winter.

Check your answers with the key on page 67.

GETTING READY FOR WINTER

VOCABULARY CHECK

knew	light	mud	nest	plants

I.   Sentences to Finish

Fill in the blank in each sentence with the correct key word from the box above.

1. My friend asked me to water her _____ while she is away.

2. Mom yelled at us because we got _____ on her kitchen floor.

3. I _____ he didn't feel well by the look on his face.

4. The room was dark so we turned on the _____ .

5. We were careful not to move the bird's _____ .

II.   Making Sense of Sentences

Put a check next to YES if the sentence makes sense. Put a check next to NO if the sentence does not make sense.

1. <u>Plants</u> are something you buy in a shoe store.   ___ YES ___ NO

2. The sun gives us <u>light</u>.   ___ YES ___ NO

3. A place for young animals is a <u>nest</u>.   ___ YES ___ NO

4. Our car needs <u>mud</u> to run.   ___ YES ___ NO

5. If I was not aware of the answer, I <u>knew</u> the answer.   ___ YES ___ NO

Check your answers with the key on page 70.

OUR WINTER HOME

PREPARATION

Key Words

asked   (ăskd)   put a question to
> *I asked the policeman for help.*

later   (lāter)   happens after the usual time
> *We left for work later than usual.*

much   (mŭch)   great in quantity
> *Much food is shared during the holidays.*

smelled   (smĕld)   used the nose
> *I smelled the pies in the bakery.*

try   (trī)   to test something
> *Try some of the salad.*

OUR WINTER HOME

Necessary Words

special   (spĕsh´- əl)   more than what is usual
                                            Today is a <u>special</u> day for me; it is my birth-
                                            day.

tomorrow   (tə - môr´ō)   the day after today
                                            I can help you <u>tomorrow</u>, but not today.

OUR WINTER HOME

Father said that we must work hard on a new house for next winter.
We must have a place to keep our things safe and dry.

Preview:
1. Read the name of the story.
2. Look at the picture.
3. Read the sentences under the picture.
4. Read the first two paragraphs of the story.
5. Then answer the following question.

You learned from your preview that the things the Robinsons left on the beach
___ a. were gone.
___ b. were wet from the winter rains.
___ c. were fine.
___ d. had caught on fire.

Turn to the Comprehension Check on page 46 for the right answer.

Now read the story.

Read to find out where the Robinsons build another home.

OUR WINTER HOME

It rained for many days. At last, it stopped. We went outside. It was spring. We felt better. Even the animals felt better.

We went to the beach. All of our things were wet. Fritz said, "Some things we can dry, but most of this is bad." I knew we must make a change. We must try to have a better home for next winter, so I looked around.

I saw a big rock near the beach. Fritz asked, "Could we make a home inside that rock?" I did not know. We would try.

I started to hit the rock. The boys asked to hit the rock. For ten days we hit the rock. We worked and worked. Jack said, "Papa! I have found a hole." Jack was right. We hit the rock even harder. Later, the hole was big enough for us to go in.

"Stop!" I said. We must be careful. The air smelled bad. We used fire to make it smell better. Soon, it was good air. We went into the rock. It was very big inside. The floor was hard. It would be a good home for the winter. We would be safe and dry.

We would build a home here. We would have a home in the rock and a home in the trees.

We caught many fish in the sea. We caught some other animals, too. We would use them for food. We saved much food for the next winter. I knew this was good, for the winters were long. We must have plenty of food. Our family was working hard.

Mother's garden was full of good things. The seeds from the ship grew. We had much good food. We ate some of it, and we saved some of it for later.

We knew we must be careful and plan for the winter.

Our new rock home was good. We built wooden walls, and we had a place for the animals. At supper I said, "This is a special day. It has been one year since we came here. We will not work tomorrow. We will give much thanks for our new home."

OUR WINTER HOME

COMPREHENSION CHECK

Preview Answer:

b. were wet from the winter rains.

Choose the best answer.

1. Fritz asked if their new home could be
   ___a. in the city.
   ___b. on a farm.
   ___c. on the beach.
   ___d. inside a rock.

2. To find out if they could make a home inside the rock, the Robinsons tried to
   ___a. blow it up.
   ___b. make a hole in it.
   ___c. dig it out of the ground.
   ___d. hide under it.

3. Before they went inside the rock, they
   ___a. made a fire to make the air smell better.
   ___b. went to town.
   ___c. went to buy paint.
   ___d. washed the rock.

4. A house inside the rock was a good idea because
   ___a. the animals liked it.
   ___b. the floor was hard.
   ___c. the Robinsons could stay dry when it rained.
   ___d. it was more fun than in a tree.

5. The family caught so many fish that they
   ___a. had a party.
   ___b. put them back into the water.
   ___c. gave some to their friends.
   ___d. saved some for the winter.

6. The Robinsons
   ___a. worked very hard together.
   ___b. were lazy.
   ___c. had someone else do their work for them.
   ___d. didn't like to do anything.

7. Not only did the Robinsons have animals and fish for food, they also had
   ___a. ice cream.
   ___b. a store nearby.
   ___c. food from Mother's garden.
   ___d. a basket of flowers.

8. Even though the Robinsons were alone on the island and had to make do with what they had, they were
   ___a. very sad.
   ___b. happy and thankful.
   ___c. hungry.
   ___d. angry about what had happened to them.

9. Another name for this story could be
   ___a. "The Rock."
   ___b. "No More Food."
   ___c. "Go Away Rain."
   ___d. "Too Little Work."

10. This story is mainly about
    ___a. buying rocks.
    ___b. Mrs. Robinson shopping for food.
    ___c. the Robinson boys learning how to cook.
    ___d. how the Robinsons plan for the next winter.

Check your answers with the key on page 67.

OUR WINTER HOME

VOCABULARY CHECK

| asked | later | much | smelled | try |

I. Sentences to Finish

Fill in the blank in each sentence with the correct key word from the box above.

1. We ate too _____ at the picnic.

2. I _____ my mother if I could go to the party.

3. Mom wants me to _____ my new dress on for Dad.

4. I can't go with you right now, but I can go_____ .

5. I _____ breakfast cooking,so I got out of bed.

II. Word Search

All the words from the box above are hidden in the puzzle below. They may be written from left to right or up and down. As you find each word, put a circle around it. One word, that is not a key word, has been done for you.

```
A   R   Z   O   T   R   Y   L
A   O   S   B   W   S   K   Z
S   A   M   T   O   M   C   H
K   C   E   N   M   U   C   H
E   X   L   A   F   T   W   O
D   A   L   R   A   J   I   N
U   V   E   I   E   R   S   L
T   I   D   L   A   T   E   R
```

Check your answers with the key on page 71.

THE PAPER

PREPARATION

Key Words

afternoon	(ăf´tər nо̄о̄n)	the time from noon to sunset *I spent all <u>afternoon</u> at the ball park.*
gave	(gāv)	past tense of give; handed over as a gift or in return of something *I <u>gave</u> the lady a ten dollar bill for the hat.*
quickly	(kwĭk lē)	as fast as possible *The girl ran <u>quickly</u> home.*
sea	(sē)	a large body of salt water *The ships at <u>sea</u> were big and full of color.*
those	(thо̄z)	to point out things spoken of *<u>Those</u> boys are my friends.*

THE PAPER

Necessary Words

learn   (lûrn)   to gain knowledge or information
> *We go to school to learn many things.*

note   (nōt)   a short piece of writing
> *I wrote you a note telling you all about my trip.*

shells   (shĕls)   hard coverings
> *At the beach, we found many kinds of shells.*

THE PAPER

The birds flew around the boat and Fritz hit one of them.

Preview: 1. Read the name of the story.
                    2. Look at the picture.
                    3. Read the sentence under the picture.
                    4. Read the first paragraph of the story.
                    5. Then answer the following question.

You learned from your preview that the Robinsons had a party because
___ a. it was Fritz's birthday.
___ b. they were going home.
___ c. they had a lot of cake.
___ d. they were on their new land one year.

Turn to the Comprehension Check on page 52 for the right answer.

Now read the story.

Read to find out about the note Fritz finds.

THE PAPER

We had a party. We ate good food, and we gave thanks. It had been one year since we came to this land. We were together and safe.

I went outside. Bad weather was coming. Soon it would rain. The rain would last a long time. We had to be ready, so we began to work. We began to get ready for the rain.

We took the things from the ship and put them in our new home. Those things had to stay dry. My children had to learn. Since they could not go to school, we took books from the ship. We put the books in our home. We would teach each other many things from those books.

We used as many things from the ship as we could. They made our home pretty. We felt very good about our home.

We stayed in our home for ten years. The boys grew big. Our lives were good. We were safe, and we were happy. But I thought, "We have been here a long time. What will become of my boys? What will happen when I am gone?" I did not know the answer.

One afternoon, Fritz went out. He took a boat and sailed around our land. He looked into the sea. The water was clear. He could see the bottom. He saw some fish and found some shells. He kept the pretty shells.

Some birds came near. They flew around the boat. Fritz hit at them and hit one of the birds. It fell into the boat. Fritz looked at the bird. Something was tied to its leg. It was a piece of paper. Fritz opened the paper. It said: "I AM A GIRL. I AM ON A ROCK. HELP ME!"

Fritz was quiet. Then the bird moved. Fritz knew what he should do, so he wrote a note: "DO NOT WORRY. HELP IS NEAR." Then he quickly tied the paper to the bird. He let the bird go. It flew away. Maybe it flew to the girl.

Fritz went home. He showed us his shells. The family wanted to get more shells, so we would go back to the sea. We would find more shells.

Later, Fritz talked only to me. He told me about the note. He told me he wanted to find the girl. I said, "You must go quickly."

A few days later, we got into the big boat. We all went to get more shells. We spent many days getting shells. When we started for home, we gave Fritz the little boat. He was not coming home with us. He was all alone, and he would look for the girl.

THE PAPER

COMPREHENSION CHECK

Choose the best answer.

1. In the beginning of this story, the Robinsons were busy getting ready because
    ___a. they were having a party.
    ___b. they were going on a boat ride.
    ___c. the rains were coming.
    ___d. they were going home.

2. Among the many things they took from the ship, were
    ___a. hats.
    ___b. swimsuits.
    ___c. shells.
    ___d. books.

3. The Robinsons
    ___a. were happy with their home.
    ___b. were tired of their home.
    ___c. were tired of each other.
    ___d. did not have a home.

4. Father wondered
    ___a. when to build another home.
    ___b. what would become of his sons.
    ___c. when someone would find them.
    ___d. what to do next.

5. One day, when Fritz was out in the boat, some birds flew around him. One bird
    ___a. bit him.
    ___b. landed on his head.
    ___c. fell into the water.
    ___d. had a paper tied to its leg.

6. The paper
    ___a. was a trick.
    ___b. was from a girl who needed help.
    ___c. fell into the water.
    ___d. blew away.

7. Fritz wrote a note telling the girl
    ___a. that help was near.
    ___b. to stay away.
    ___c. he couldn't help her.
    ___d. he was lost, too.

8. Fritz told only his father about the note because
    ___a. he did not care about the girl.
    ___b. he could not read the note.
    ___c. he did not want his family to worry when he went to look for the girl.
    ___d. he did not talk to his brothers anymore.

9. Another name for this story could be
    ___a. "The Shells."
    ___b. "Too Many Books."
    ___c. "Back to the Tree House."
    ___d. "Fritz Finds A Note."

10. This story is mainly about
    ___a. the many kinds of shells on the beach.
    ___b. Fritz going off on his own to find a girl.
    ___c. how to catch a bird.
    ___d. Fritz not going to school.

Check your answers with the key on page 67.

THE PAPER

VOCABULARY CHECK

| afternoon | gave | quickly | sea | those |

I. Sentences to Finish

Fill in the blank in each sentence with the correct key word from the box above.

1. John _____ this yellow flower to me.

2. I ran _____ up the stairs after my cat.

3. Did you see _____ pretty butterflies?

4. My little brother sleeps for an hour every_____ .

5. Ships are used to move people and things across the _____ .

II. Matching

Write the letter of the correct meaning from Column B next to the key word in Column A.

Column A

1. gave _____

2. those _____

3. afternoon _____

4. quickly _____

5. sea _____

Column B

a. a large body of salt water

b. handed over as a gift

c. as fast as possible

d. to point out things spoken of

e. the time from noon to sunset

Check your answers with the key on page 71.

JENNY

PREPARATION

Key Words

across	(ə krôs)	from the other side of *We live <u>across</u> the road from you.*
doing	(do͞o ing)	to perform, to act out *What is that girl <u>doing</u>?*
every	(ĕv´ rē)	each one in a group of people or things; all *<u>Every</u> student must report to the gym.*
nothing	(nŭth´ ĭng)	not anything; not at all *The doctor found <u>nothing</u> wrong with John.*
part	(pärt)	a portion; something less than all *<u>Part</u> of my day is spent in my car.*

JENNY

Necessary Words

canoe   (kə - n$\overline{oo}$)   a small boat
> *When the <u>canoe</u> tipped over, I fell into the water.*

cave   (kāv)   a hollow space under the ground; an opening in the side of a hill, mountain, etc.
> *We were surprised to find the <u>cave</u> hidden by the bushes.*

storm   (stŏrm)   strong wind, rain and lightning
> *We could tell by the dark sky that a <u>storm</u> was coming.*

JENNY

Jenny tells Fritz about herself.

Preview: 1. Read the name of the story.
2. Look at the picture.
3. Read the sentence under the picture.
4. Read the first paragraph of the story.
5. Then answer the following question.

You learned from your preview that, after several days, Fritz
___ a. came back home.
___ b. was lost.
___ c. found the girl.
___ d. was tired and hungry.

Turn to the Comprehension Check on page 58 for the right answer.

Now read the story.

Read to find out about Jenny.

JENNY

Fritz went in the little boat. He sailed for days. He looked in every place, but saw nothing. Then he saw someone. He took his boat to the beach. Someone came toward him. It was a girl.

Fritz said, "Hello. My name is Fritz. I got your note. I came to help you." The girl said, "Hello. My name is Jenny. I am glad you have come."

Fritz and Jenny sat down. They ate some food. Then Jenny told her story. Jenny said, "My mother is dead. I was on a ship with my father when our ship was in a storm. I could not find my father. I was in a little boat and, for many days, I was lost. I came here. I am all alone. I have just a few things, so I sent the note." Fritz said, "You were smart to send the note. You found food. You are very brave for doing that."

Back home, we were scared. We had heard nothing, and we missed Fritz. He was part of us. We went in our boat to find Fritz. We saw a big fish in the water, so we went around it.

We saw a man in a canoe. We could not see who it was or what he was doing. When we started to go to the boat, the man moved away. Then Jack shouted across to the man. The man came to us. It was Fritz.

At first, he thought we were bad men. He was glad Jack called to him. He told us about Jenny and took us to her.

Jenny came back with us. She became part of our family. It was a good time for every one of us.

We went inside the cave for winter. Since we were happy, the time went by fast.

Soon, it was spring. One day, while we were outside, Jack and Franz were playing. They were making a lot of noise. Then we heard some more noise. It was from the sea. The noise was coming from a ship. We went inside to hide because bad men could be on the ship. We slept very little that night.

In the morning, we went outside. Fritz and I looked at the ship. Hooray! It was a ship with good men. They were here to help us. We went across the beach. We went on the ship. What would they think of us?

JENNY

COMPREHENSION CHECK

Choose the best answer.

Preview Answer:
c. found the girl.

1. Jenny told Fritz that
   ___a. she liked him.
   ___b. she was afraid.
   ___c. she did not need his help.
   ___d. she was also in a storm at sea.

2. Fritz told Jenny that
   ___a. he liked her.
   ___b. she was brave.
   ___c. he was afraid.
   ___d. he did not like his family.

3. Back home, the Robinsons
   ___a. did not miss Fritz at all.
   ___b. were glad he left.
   ___c. were scared because Fritz was gone so long.
   ___d. were fighting with one another.

4. When the Robinsons were looking for Fritz, they spotted someone in the water. Who was it?
   ___a. Jenny's father.
   ___b. Jenny.
   ___c. Mother.
   ___d. Fritz.

5. First, Fritz took his family to see Jenny. Then,
   ___a. Jenny went to live with them.
   ___b. Jenny went home.
   ___c. Jenny's father came to get her.
   ___d. Jenny and Fritz got married.

6. One spring day, the Robinsons heard some noise. The noise was from
   ___a. a passing train.
   ___b. the dogs.
   ___c. a ship.
   ___d. some birds.

7. At first, the Robinsons were afraid of the ship, so they hid. The next day, they
   ___a. ran away for good.
   ___b. found out the ship had come to help them.
   ___c. threw things at the ship.
   ___d. called the police.

8. The Robinsons were afraid that
   ___a. the men on the ship would hurt them.
   ___b. they would have to feed all the people on the ship.
   ___c. they would have to leave their land.
   ___d. the ship would be lost in a storm.

9. Another name for this story could be
   ___a. "The Turtle."
   ___b. "The Winter."
   ___c. "My Little Boat."
   ___d. "Help At Last."

10. This story is mainly about
    ___a. the Robinsons hiding.
    ___b. the Robinsons finding other people.
    ___c. Jenny going away.
    ___d. Jenny missing her father.

Check your answers with the key on page 67.

This page may be reproduced for classroom use.

JENNY

VOCABULARY CHECK

across	doing	every	nothing	part

I. Sentences to Finish

Fill in the blank in each sentence with the correct key word from the box above.

1. You should brush your teeth three times _____ day.

2. I am not going _____ the street without you.

3. The dog ate only _____ of my homework.

4. Why are you _____ that?

5. There was _____ to do at work, so I went home.

II. Crossword Puzzle

Use the words from the box above to fill in the puzzle. The meanings below help you choose the right words.

Across

1. less than all
2. not anything

Down

1. each one in a group
2. acting out
3. from the other side of

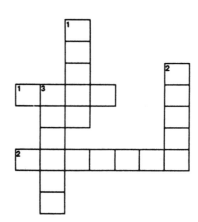

Check your answers with the key on page 71.

This page may be reproduced for classroom use.

GOOD-BY

PREPARATION

Key Words

apart	(ə pärt)	at a distance; not together *Keep those two animals apart.*
asleep	(ə slēp)	sleeping *Dad fell asleep on the sofa.*
bedroom	(bĕd´rōōm)	a room for sleeping *My brother and I share a bedroom.*
behind	(bǐ hīnd)	to the rear; in back of *I sat behind the driver.*
table	(tā´bəl)	furniture with a flat top and legs *The plates and cups are on the table.*

GOOD-BY

Necessary Words

captain (kăp´tən) the boss of a ship
> *The <u>captain</u> greeted everyone who came onto the ship.*

changed (chănjd) made different; not the same anymore
> *Everyone liked the way I <u>changed</u> my hair.*

share (shâr) hand out fairly
> *Each one of us did his <u>share</u> of the work.*

strong (strông) able to last; having much power; not easily changed
> *John is not as <u>strong</u> as I, so Mother asked me to help him.*

GOOD-BY

The captain was surprised to hear our story.

Preview: 1. Read the name of the story.
2. Look at the picture.
3. Read the sentence under the picture.
4. Read the first paragraph of the story.
5. Then answer the following question.

You learned from your preview that
___ a. the ship was looking for Jenny.
___ b. the ship was lost.
___ c. the ship was sinking.
___ d. the ship was in trouble.

Turn to the Comprehension Check on page 64 for the right answer.

Now read the story.

Read to find out what happens to the Robinson family.

GOOD-BY

The captain was glad to see us. He knew Jenny's father. The ship was looking for Jenny. Her father would be very happy because they would no longer be apart. This made Fritz feel good.

The captain and his men came to our home. They sat at our table. They were surprised to see all that we had done. We showed them around our land. They liked our place. Some of them said they wanted to stay here. We said yes. Our home was changed. We were lost no more. Now our place would have more people.

That night, when everyone was asleep, Mother and I went to our bedroom. I spoke with Mother. "Fritz will leave with Jenny. Franz wants to go to school, so he will go back, too. Jack and Ernest want to stay behind with us. Our family will be apart. What do you want?"

Mother said, "I love our place. If you will stay, I will stay." I also wanted to stay in our new home because I loved it, too. Then we fell asleep in our bedroom.

Later on, we had a party. We sat around a big table. We were happy for all our new friends. We helped them get ready to leave. I gave Fritz the nice things we found so he would have the money to start his new life back home. Fritz said he loved Jenny. I told him to ask Jenny's father if he could marry her. Jenny was happy. We were happy. We all loved Jenny.

On the night before they left us behind, I gave Fritz this story. I said, "As you know, I wrote this story for my children. I hope that it can help other children. Take this with you. Share it with other young people. They might learn something. They might learn about being brave. They might learn about being strong. They might learn that working together with those they love, makes a better life for all."

I said good-by to this story, to Jenny and Fritz, and to Franz. I wished for them to be forever happy. I knew Fritz would take good care of my story.

GOOD-BY

COMPREHENSION CHECK

Choose the best answer.

Preview Answer:

a. the ship was looking for Jenny.

1. Jenny's father would be very happy because
   ___a. Jenny left home.
   ___b. he and Jenny would no longer be apart.
   ___c. Jenny was living with the Robinsons.
   ___d. the ship's captain was happy.

2. When the captain and his men saw what the Robinsons did on their land, they
   ___a. laughed at them.
   ___b. felt sorry for them.
   ___c. said they liked their place.
   ___d. told the Robinsons they were in trouble.

3. The Robinsons felt their home was changed because
   ___a. some of the people from the ship were going to stay on their land.
   ___b. stores were being built.
   ___c. apartments were being built.
   ___d. the people from the ship were making a lot of noise.

4. Jenny was going home to her father. Who else was going back with her?
   ___a. Fritz and Franz.
   ___b. Mother.
   ___c. Father.
   ___d. Jack and Ernest.

5. Fritz wanted to go back with Jenny because
   ___a. he did not like his mother and father.
   ___b. he loved her.
   ___c. he was tired of their home.
   ___d. he wanted to find a job.

6. Franz wanted to go back on the ship because
   ___a. he wanted to marry Jenny.
   ___b. he hated his mother.
   ___c. he did not like living in a tree house.
   ___d. he wanted to go to school.

7. Mr. Robinson asked Mrs. Robinson if she wanted to leave their new land. She said
   ___a. she was tired of the tree house.
   ___b. she was going to live with Fritz and Jenny.
   ___c. no, she loved it here.
   ___d. no, because she did not want to go on another ship.

8. Mr. Robinson gave something very special to Fritz to take back home with him. What was it?
   ___a. This story.
   ___b. Some money.
   ___c. Some clothes.
   ___d. A new car.

9. Another name for this story could be
   ___a. "A Happy Ending."
   ___b. "Another Sinking Ship."
   ___c. "New Dishes."
   ___d. "Please Write."

10. This story is mainly about
    ___a. Jenny's father coming to get her.
    ___b. Fritz and Jenny fighting.
    ___c. the Robinson family going home.
    ___d. what happens to the Robinsons when they are found.

Check your answers with the key on page 67.

This page may be reproduced for classroom use.

GOOD-BY

VOCABULARY CHECK

| apart | asleep | bedroom | behind | table |

I.   Sentences to Finish

Fill in the blank in each sentence with the correct key word from the box above.

1. My brother sleeps in the same _____ as I do.

2. I have to set the _____ every night.

3. The flowers _____ our house are very pretty.

4. While I was reading, I fell _____ .

5. I had to take the toy _____ to find out why it wouldn't work.

II.   Mixed-Up Words

First, unscramble the letters in Column A to spell out the key words. Then, match the key words with the right meaning in Column B by drawing a line.

Column A

1. balet   _____

2. broomed   _____

3. tarpa   _____

4. pleeas   _____

5. hinbed   _____

Column B

a. a room for sleeping

b. not together

c. sleeping

d. to the rear

e. a piece of furniture that has a flat top and legs

Check your answers with the key on page 72.

NOTES

COMPREHENSION CHECK ANSWER KEY
Lessons CTR-104-31 to CTR-104-40

LESSON NUMBER	QUESTION NUMBER										PAGE NUMBER
	1	2	3	4	5	6	7	8	9	10	
CTR-A-31	a	c	b	d	c	a	c	ⓓ	△a	[b]	10
CTR-A-32	a	c	b	d	b	c	a	ⓑ	△a	[d]	16
CTR-A-33	c	d	a	b	a	d	a	ⓑ	△d	[c]	22
CTR-A-34	d	c	b	a	c	a	b	ⓓ	△d	[c]	28
CTR-A-35	b	c	d	a	d	c	b	ⓐ	△d	[a]	34
CTR-A-36	d	a	c	a	b	c	ⓐ	d	△c	[d]	40
CTR-A-37	d	b	a	c	d	a	c	ⓑ	△a	[d]	46
CTR-A-38	c	d	a	b	d	b	a	ⓒ	△d	[b]	52
CTR-A-39	d	b	c	d	a	c	b	ⓐ	△d	[b]	58
CTR-A-40	b	c	a	a	b	d	c	ⓐ	△a	[d]	64

◯ = Inference (not said straight out, but you know from what is said)

△ = Another name for the story

▢ = Main idea of the story

NOTES

VOCABULARY CHECK ANSWER KEY

Lessons CTR A-31 to CTR A-40

I.
1. swim
2. ship
3. beach
4. through
5. found

II.
1. NO
2. YES
3. NO
4. NO
5. YES

I.
1. running
2. monkey
3. people
4. sleep
5. began

II.

H	L	S	B	D	K	J	M
M	O	N	K	E	Y	X	P
B	E	G	A	N	S	V	E
O	J	K	B	D	L	Z	O
M	C	L	O	T	E	T	P
S	V	D	D	T	E	Q	L
U	W	F	Q	U	P	R	E
T	R	U	N	N	I	N	G

I.
1. Our
2. hurt
3. trees
4. today
5. boat

II.
1. c
2. e
3. a
4. b
5. d

VOCABULARY CHECK ANSWER KEY

Lessons CTR A-31 to CTR A-40

34   OUR TREE HOUSE   29

I. 1. ready
    2. roof
    3. idea
    4. these
    5. pulled

II.

```
              ¹t
              h  ²i
¹p  u  l  l  e  d
              s  e
           ³r e  a  d  y
              o
              o
              f
```

35   BACK TO THE SHIP   35

I. 1. turtle
    2. daily
    3. watch
    4. everywhere
    5. waited

II. 1. watch, c
    2. turtle, e
    3. waited, d
    4. daily, b
    5. everywhere, a

36   GETTING READY FOR WINTER   41

I. 1. plants
    2. mud
    3. knew
    4. light
    5. nest

II. 1. NO
    2. YES
    3. YES
    4. NO
    5. NO

VOCABULARY CHECK ANSWER KEY

Lessons CTR A-31 to CTR A-40

LESSON
NUMBER

PAGE
NUMBER

37   OUR WINTER HOME   47

I.   1. much
     2. asked
     3. try
     4. later
     5. smelled

II.

A	R	Z	O	T	R	Y	L
A	O	S	B	W	S	K	Z
S	A	M	T	O	M	C	H
K	C	E	N	M	U	C	H
E	X	L	A	F	T	W	O
D	A	L	R	A	J	I	N
U	V	E	I	E	R	S	L
T	I	D	L	A	T	E	R

38   THE PAPER   53

I.   1. gave
     2. quickly
     3. those
     4. afternoon
     5. sea

II. 1. b
     2. d
     3. e
     4. c
     5. a

39   JENNY   59

I.   1. every
     2. across
     3. part
     4. doing
     5. nothing

II.

```
              e
              v
              e
  p  a  r  t
              d
     c  y     o
     r        i
  n  o  t  h  i  n  g
     s
     s
```

71

VOCABULARY CHECK ANSWER KEY

Lessons CTR A-31 to CTR A-40

LESSON
NUMBER

PAGE
NUMBER

40   ALONE AT SEA   65

I. 1. bedroom   II. 1. table, e
    2. table   2. bedroom, a
    3. behind   3. apart, b
    4. asleep   4. asleep, c
    5. apart   5. behind, d